# BIG CAT

# BIG CAT

by **Ethan Long**

I
Like to
Read®

Holiday House / New York

Library of Congress Cataloging-in-Publication Data
Long, Ethan, author, illustrator.
Big Cat / by Ethan Long. — First edition.
pages cm. — (I like to read)
Summary: A hefty feline puts up with all kinds of indignities
from the children in her loving but rambunctious family.
ISBN 978-0-8234-3538-8 (hardcover)
[1. Cats—Fiction. 2. Family life—Fiction.] I. Title.
PZ7.L8453Bi 2016
[E]—dc23
2015014875

ISBN 978-0-8234-3539-5 (paperback)

To our cat, Bailey,
aka Kit-T, aka Skunk,
the best cat
on the planet

Big Cat can nap.

Big Cat can wake.

Big Cat can hug.

Big Cat can fly.

Big Cat can hide.

Big Cat can dance.

Big Cat can be fun.

Big Cat can sit.

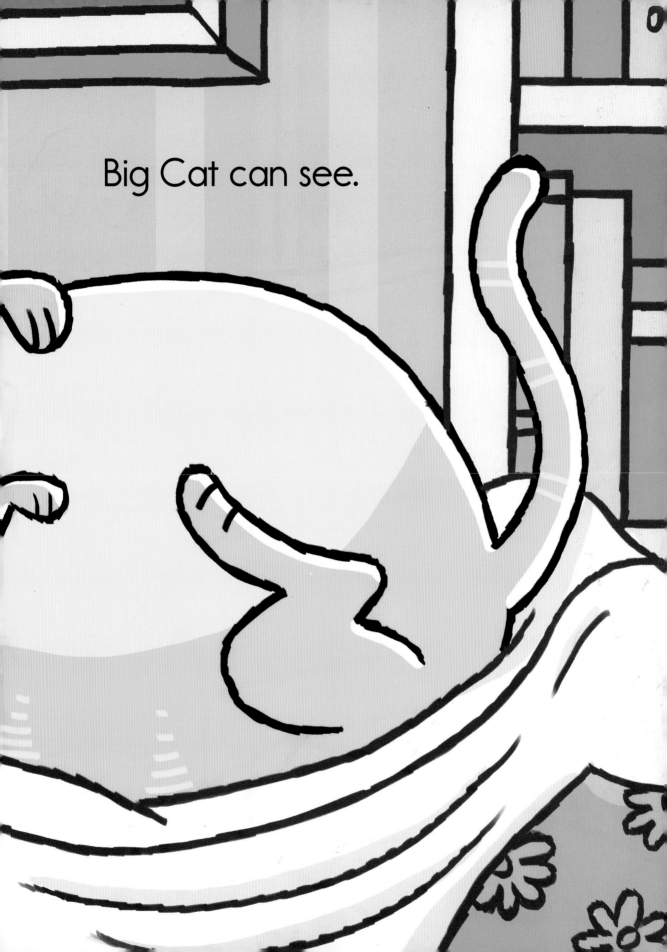

Big Cat can see.

Big Cat can run.

Big Cat can be fun.